In memory of Grandma Louisa,
my star forever ~ C.N.

First published 2008 by Macmillan Children's Books
This edition published 2009 by Macmillan Children's Books
a division of Macmillan Publishers Limited
20 New Wharf Road, London N1 9RR
Basingstoke and Oxford
Associated companies throughout the world
www.panmacmillan.com

ISBN: 978-1-4050-3507-1

Text copyright © Carl Norac 2008
Illustrations copyright © Ingrid Godon 2008
Moral rights asserted

1 3 5 7 9 8 6 4 2

A CIP catalogue record for this book
is available from the British Library.

Printed in Belgium

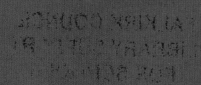

My Grandma is a STAR

CARL
NORAC

INGRID
GODON

MACMILLAN CHILDREN'S BOOKS

My grandma is a star.
She twinkles brightly,
just for me.

My grandma is a sun.
When she's close to me,
I'm never cold.

But sometimes she's a meteor.

At the supermarket her trolley goes faster than anyone else's. It looks like it's flying!

My grandma's favourite thing
is flowers. She'd fill the whole
universe with them if she could!

She loves travelling, too.
She'll go anywhere.

If someone organised a holiday in
outer space she'd be the first to go.

My grandma is a gymnast.
She's super bendy.

Once I even saw her walk on her hands!

My grandma is a queen and
the kitchen is her palace.
When she cooks my favourite meal,
I give her a gold paper crown.

I always feel important when
I'm with my grandma.

I like it when she says,
"How are you, my little prince?"

Sometimes my grandma
is a clown.

She pretends to be asleep —
but then she throws a cushion,
and our battle begins.
We laugh and laugh!

My grandma is also
a secret agent.

When we play hide-and-seek
she keeps so still and quiet
that I can never find her!

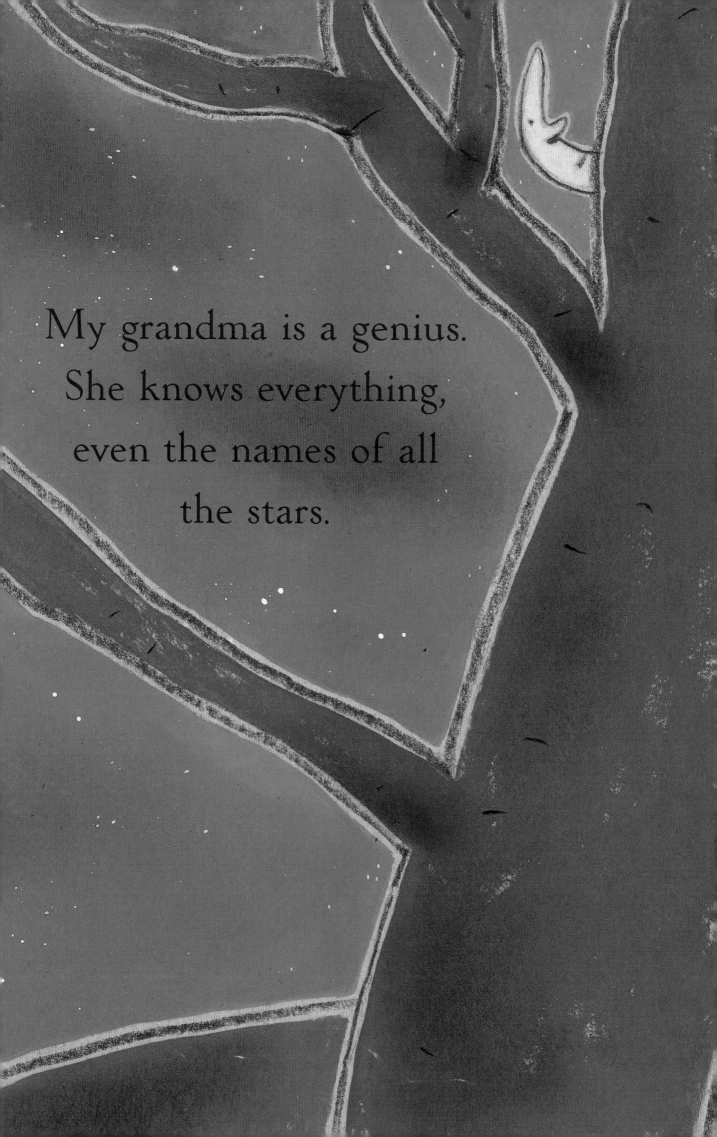

My grandma is a genius.
She knows everything,
even the names of all
the stars.

She tells me a new secret
about the world every day.

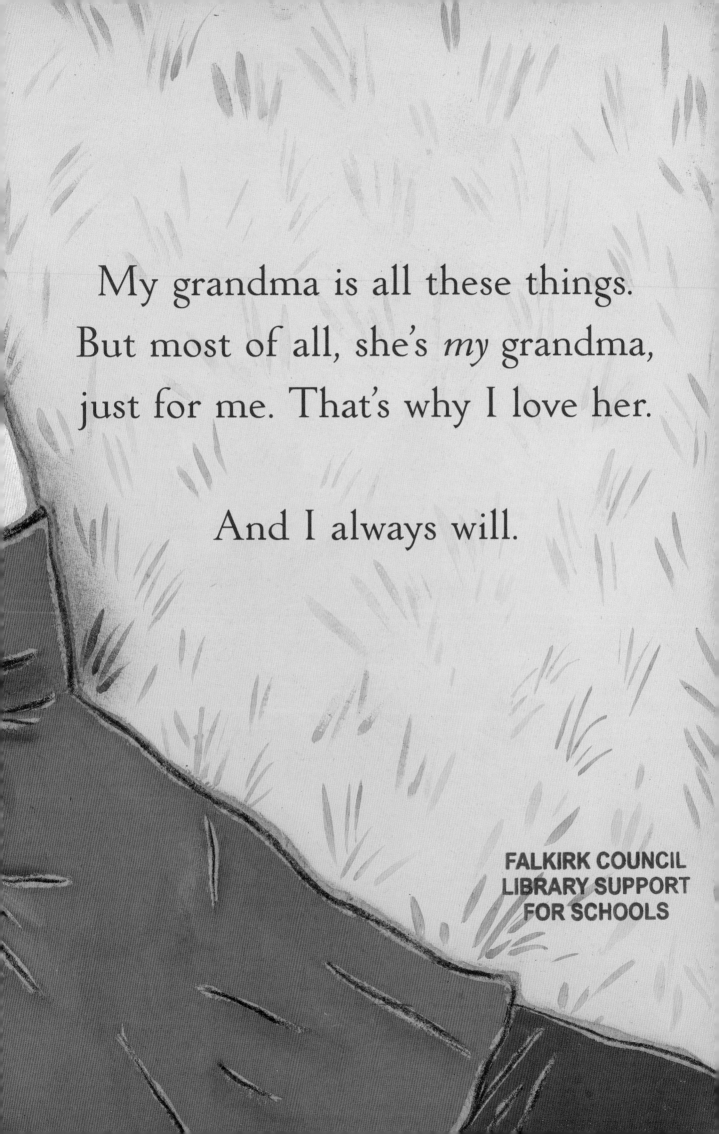

My grandma is all these things.
But most of all, she's *my* grandma,
just for me. That's why I love her.

And I always will.